RED FOX

For Avril with love – JC

For Will – MMcQ

Other books illustrated by Mary McQuillan:

Our Twitchy *by Kes Gray*

Who Will Sing My Puff-a-bye? *by Charlotte Hudson*

In a Little While *by Charlotte Hudson*

Squeaky Clean *by Simon Puttock*

DIPPY'S SLEEPOVER
A RED FOX BOOK
978 1 849 41212 4

First published in Great Britain by The Bodley Head,
an imprint of Random House Children's Books

Bodley Head edition published 2006
Red Fox edition published 2006

5 7 9 10 8 6

Red Fox Books are published by Random House Children's Books,
61–63 Uxbridge Road, London W5 5SA, A Random House Group Company.
Addresses for companies within The Random House Group Limited can be found
at: www.randomhouse.co.uk/offices.htm

THE RANDOM HOUSE GROUP Limited Reg. No. 954009
www.**kids**at**randomhouse**.co.uk

A CIP catalogue record for this book is available from the British Library.

Printed in China

On Tuesday after school, Dippy rushed home. "Spike's invited me to sleep at his house on Friday!" he squeaked, wagging his tail excitedly. "We'll watch *Scarysaurs Go Wild* and eat popfern and . . ."

Dippy's tail wagged

harder and
harder
and harder . . .

"Great!" said Mrs Diplodocus.

". . . and we'll go to bed late and
switch on our torches,
and . . . and . . ."

Dippy's tail stopped wagging.
"I can't go," he said sadly.
"Why not?" asked Mum.
"Because when I'm asleep,"
Dippy said, "I wet the bed."

Mrs Diplodocus wrapped her long neck around Dippy and gave him a hug. "Lots of podlets wet the bed," she said. "Mrs Triceratops will understand. She can put rubber sheets on the mattress. I'll phone her."

"Spike mustn't know
I wet the bed!"
said Dippy.
"I'll be *dry*
by Friday!"

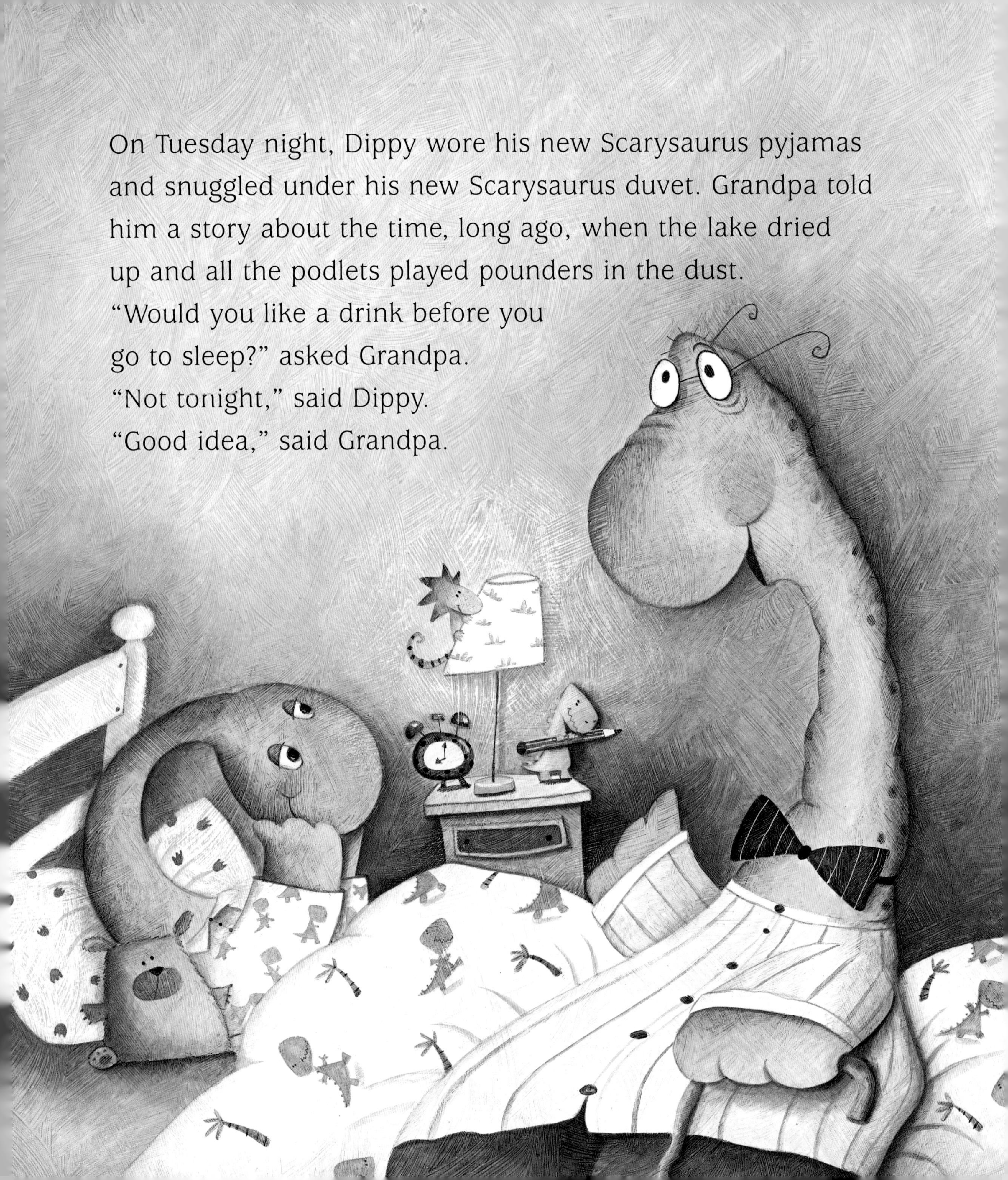

On Tuesday night, Dippy wore his new Scarysaurus pyjamas and snuggled under his new Scarysaurus duvet. Grandpa told him a story about the time, long ago, when the lake dried up and all the podlets played pounders in the dust.

"Would you like a drink before you go to sleep?" asked Grandpa.

"Not tonight," said Dippy.

"Good idea," said Grandpa.

Dippy went to sleep and dreamed
of playing pounders in the dust.

But in the middle of the night, in the
middle of the dusty dried-up lake . . .

. . . a stream began to trickle . . .

On Wednesday morning,
Mrs Diplodocus changed the bedding.
"Friday will be here soon," she said.
"Let me phone Spike's mother."

"Spike mustn't know I wet the bed!"
said Dippy.

"I'll be dry by Friday!"

On Wednesday night, Dippy wore his Little Pterrors pyjamas and snuggled under his Little Pterrors duvet. Dad read him a story about a hot dry desert where podlets played slide and squeak down the sand dunes.

"I'll go to the toilet before you turn off the light," said Dippy.
"Good idea," said Dad.

Dippy went to sleep and dreamed of playing
slide and squeak down desert sand dunes.

But in the middle of the night,
in the middle of the desert . . .

. . . a water hole began to fill . . .

On Thursday morning,
Mrs Diplodocus changed the bedding.
"It's Friday tomorrow," she said.
"I should phone Spike's mother."

"Spike mustn't know I wet the bed!"
said Dippy.

"I'll be dry by Friday!"

On Thursday night, Dippy had to wear his old cavebear pyjamas and snuggle under his old cavebear duvet, because everything else was in the wash. Mum got out the album and they laughed at the photo of Dippy buried in the sand.
"Wake me up when you go to bed," said Dippy,
"so I can go to the toilet."
"Good idea,' said Mum,
and she did.

Dippy went to sleep and dreamed
he was buried in the sand.
But in the middle of the night,
in the middle of the beach . . .

. . . the tide began to come in . . .

On Friday morning, Mrs Diplodocus changed the bedding. Then she packed Dippy's Scarysaurus pyjamas for him to take to Spike's house after school. "I'm phoning Spike's mother now," she said, but Mrs Triceratops had already gone out.

"Phew!" Dippy said. "Spike mustn't know I wet the bed! I'll be dry tonight!"

On Friday after school, Dippy had a great time at Spike's house. Mrs Triceratops made them deep-fried ferns for tea. They watched *Scarysaurs Go Wild* and ate popfern and drank firconeade.

"It's time to go to bed now," said Mrs Triceratops.
"Would you like another drink?"
"No thanks," said Dippy and Spike together.

Dippy and Spike put on their matching Scarysaurus pyjamas and snuggled under their matching Scarysaurus duvets with their cuddly cavebears. Dippy was very tired, but he didn't want to go to sleep in case he wet the bed.

"Let's stay awake all night!" he yawned.
"Good idea!" Spike yawned back.
They switched on their torches, but
soon their eyelids began to droop.

Dippy and Spike fell asleep and
dreamed scary dreams
about Scarysaurs.

A huge Scarysaurus was chasing them through the snow. It was just about to catch them!

But in the middle of the night, in the middle of the volcano . . .

. . . the snow
began to melt . . .

On Saturday morning, Mrs Triceratops
changed both sets of bedding.
"I didn't want you to know that I wet the bed!"
Dippy told Spike as a blush rippled down
his long neck.
"Well, *I* didn't want *you* to know
that I wet the bed," said Spike,
whose horn had gone all pink.

They looked at each other and smiled wobbly smiles.
"Don't worry about it," Mrs Triceratops said.
"You'll grow out of it. Lots of podlets
wet the bed!"

"How did you get on at Spike's?"
Mum asked Dippy when he got home.
"It was great," said Dippy. "We watched
Scarysaurs Go Wild and ate popfern and . . . "
Dippy's tail
wagged
harder
and harder
and harder . . .

"And the bed . . . ?" asked Mum.
"Don't worry about that," said Dippy.
"Spike wets the bed, too!"
"Does he?" Mum smiled.
"Yes," Dippy said. "Lots of podlets wet the bed. We'll grow out of it."
"Of course you will," said Mum, giving him a huge hug.

On Saturday night Dippy fell into a deep sleep, and on Sunday morning . . .

Mrs Diplodocus didn’t have to change the bedding!